For my sweet Gram, whose garden still grows. —D.P.

To my Aaron, my cats and my Mom! —A.B.

Library of Congress Cataloging-in-Publication Data

Names: Prochovnic, Dawn Babb, author. | Brereton, Alice, illustrator.
Title: Lucy's blooms / written by Dawn Babb Prochovnic; illustrated by Alice Brereton.
Description: [Berkeley]: West Margin Press, [2021] | Audience: Ages 6–9. | Audience: Grades 2–3. | Summary: Lucy wants to surprise her grandmother by winning a blue ribbon at the flower show, and after a few mistakes she is proud of her results, but will the judges agree?
Identifiers: LCCN 2020046913 (print) | LCCN 2020046914 (ebook) | ISBN 9781513267197 (hardback) | ISBN 9781513267203 (ebook)
Subjects: CYAC: Gardening—Fiction. | Wild flowers—Fiction. | Grandmothers—Fiction. | Contests—Fiction.
Classification: LCC PZ7.1.P773 Luc 2021 (print) | LCC PZ7.1.P773 (ebook) | DDC [E]—dc23
LC record available at https://lccn.loc.gov/2020046913
LC ebook record available at https://lccn.loc.gov/2020046914

Proudly distributed by Ingram Publisher Services

Printed in China
25 24 23 22 21 1 2 3 4 5

Published by West Margin Press

WEST
MARGIN
PRESS

WestMarginPress.com

WEST MARGIN PRESS
Publishing Director: Jennifer Newens
Marketing Manager: Angela Zbornik
Project Specialist: Micaela Clark
Editor: Olivia Ngai
Design & Production: Rachel Lopez Metzger

Lucy's Blooms

Written by Dawn Babb Prochovnic

Illustrated by Alice Brereton

WEST
MARGIN
PRESS

Lucy wove her wagon through the meadow behind Gram's house. She breathed in the soft, sweet smell as hundreds and hundreds of bright, yellow blooms danced tall and proud in the wild grass.

While Lucy wandered, she sang Gram's gardening song.

"Load up the wagon and off we go. Plant little seeds and watch them grow…"

A clump of blooms leaned in to listen.

Lucy stopped and smiled.
"Hello there," she said.
"Would you like to enter
a flower contest? We could
surprise Gram with a new
blue ribbon!"

The blooms swayed in the breeze as if to nod their approval.

"First, I need to move you," Lucy said as she gently shoveled the blooms out of the ground and into a cozier spot. She scooped handfuls of soil until the flowerpot was full.

The blooms stood still.

"Now wait here," Lucy said, patting down the last bit of soil. "The Flower Festival is in three days, but I'll come back to visit you tomorrow."

Lucy danced tall and proud, just like the blooms in the meadow, all the way back to Gram's house.

"Oh my, what a lively show," said Gram, clapping her hands. "You must be ready for a cool drink after all that whirling and waving."

While Gram poured the pitcher, she whistled a song. Lucy stood close to listen.

The blooms dug their roots into the soil and explored their new surroundings. But as the day lingered on, the soil grew dry and the blooms began to fade.

The next morning, Lucy returned to find her blooms drooping over the side of their pot.

"Oh no," she said. "You must be thirsty. Let's get you some water." Lucy lifted her watering can and sprinkled her blooms. While Lucy watered, she whistled a song.

Her blooms perked up to listen.

"Much better," said Lucy. "I'll come back first thing tomorrow to give you another drink."

Lucy skipped back to the house to draw pictures of her blooms for Gram.

"Oh my, what a cheery bunch," said Gram. "And I'll bet they're hardy too. Did I ever tell you the story about the daisies I knew that liked to play hide-and-seek?"

Lucy nestled next to Gram on the porch swing to listen.

The blooms tried to nap in the meadow, but the blazing sun was too bright. The next day when Lucy returned, she found her blooms curled and crisp.

"Oh no," said Lucy. "You must be uncomfortable. Maybe you'd like a shadier spot."

She wheeled the wagon under
the old oak tree and climbed
onto Gram's tire swing.

"Did you know that once upon a time Gram played hide-and-seek with some daisies?"

Her blooms peeked their sunny faces out to listen.

"Ah, much better," said Lucy, when her story was finished. "I'll come back first thing tomorrow to take you to the contest."

Lucy skipped back to the house and snuggled under a blanket to watch the sunset with Gram.

"Oh my, this is my favorite part," said Gram.

"Mine too," said Lucy.

The blooms shivered in the cool evening air. The next morning, Lucy's blooms huddled together in the center of their pot.

"Oh no," said Lucy. "You must have been too cold last night."

Lucy brought her blooms
out into the sun.

She sprinkled more
water on her blooms.

She whistled more
songs to her blooms.

She told more stories
to her blooms.

Then she danced a little
dance for her blooms.

Lucy's blooms bobbed playfully
as they basked in Lucy's love.

"Much better," said Lucy. "Now you're ready to win!"

Lucy rolled her wagon down the
path and into the town square.

The judges looked at Lucy's blooms.

They sniffed at Lucy's blooms.

They measured
Lucy's blooms.

Then one of the judges
opened the rulebook and
pointed to the small print.

"Ah-ha!" she said. "These are a bunch of weeds."

"And as the rulebook says, 'No weeds allowed,'" another judge said.

Lucy wilted.

The weeds went white.

"Tough break, kid," said the first judge.

"Better luck next time," said another, as they moved on to the prize table.

Lucy watched as the winners were announced:

"Most Beautiful." "Most Fragrant." "Most Colorful."

She stood by her blooms and breathed in their soft, sweet smell. Their cottony tufts tickled her nose. "Don't worry," Lucy said. "You win the Grand Prize: Most Loved!"

Her blooms shimmered in the sun.

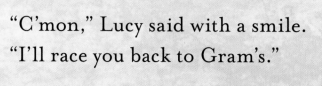

"C'mon," Lucy said with a smile.
"I'll race you back to Gram's."

She took hold of her wagon and ran.

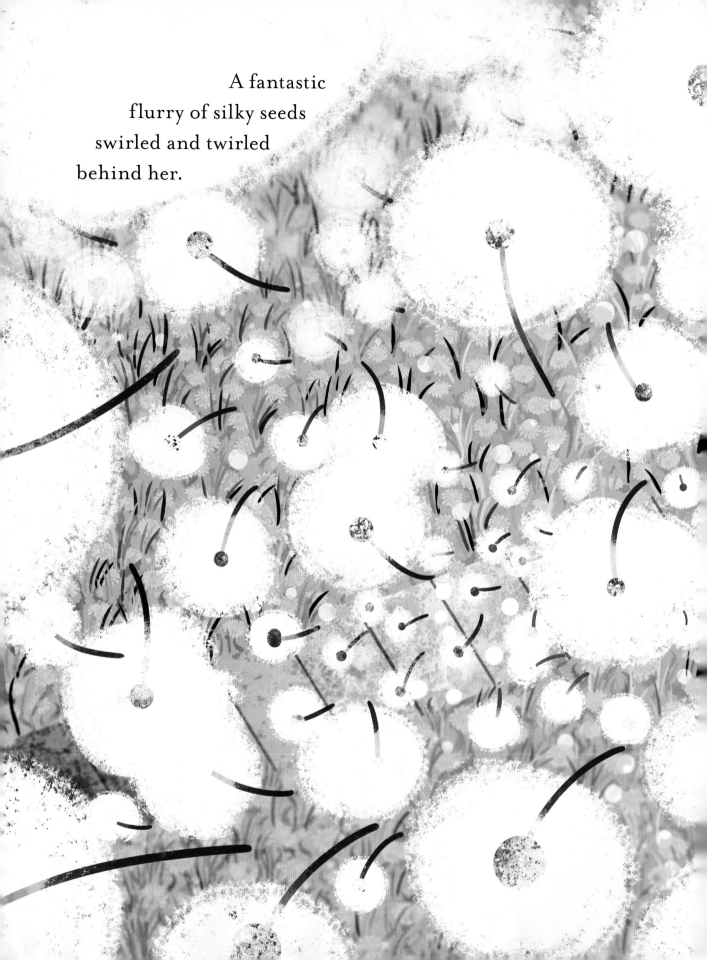

A fantastic
flurry of silky seeds
swirled and twirled
behind her.